Arianne Carson has always enjoyed reading and writing, when she was diagnosed with GAD (General Anxiety Disorder) and depression, writing was an invaluable source of comfort. Arianne wrote her poetry in order for her to understand and evaluate those thoughts and feelings.

To my family and friends for supporting and loving me even when I was at my lowest point.

Arianne M Carson

HIDDEN FEELINGS

AUSTIN MACAULEY PUBLISHERS™

LONDON • CAMBRIDGE • NEW YORK • SHARJAH

A CIP catalogue record for this title is available from the British Library.

ISBN 9781528917353 (Paperback)
ISBN 9781528930604 (ePub e-book)

www.austinmacauley.com

First Published (2020)
Austin Macauley Publishers Ltd
25 Canada Square
Canary Wharf
London
E14 5LQ

To my wonderful and supportive family, especially my parents for supporting me and loving me no matter what I do. You are the reason I still go on, each and every day.

To the staff that looked after me at CAMHS, for never judging me and creating a safe space to let out my demons.

To the English Department for always letting me sit and read in the corridor during my breaks.

To my wonderful friends for accepting me and making me feel important for the last five years.

That Girl That You Know

That Girl You Know
The one in your class
Her blonde hair shining and blue eyes glistening
Always happy to talk and laugh
That Girl You Know

That Girl You Know, has gone quiet as a mouse
Forever wishing to be at her house
That Girl You Know, her blonde hair now brown
Her glistening blue eyes now dull
And some say she has turned cold
That Girl You Know

That Girl You Know
The one on your bus or train covering her arms
In jumpers and long sleeves, even in summer
Saying that she was 'feeling cold'
Which was one of the biggest lies she ever told
That Girl You Know

That Girl You Know
The one you always ask to do homework
Whilst you sit back and smirk
That Girl You Know under constant stress
Always trying to do her best
That Girl You Know

That Girl You Know
The one who finds comfort in a corridor
The one you see reading
The one you are constantly teasing
That Girl You Know

That Girl You Know
The one you made build her walls so high, nobody could take them down
Her smile is in a permeant frown
That Girl You Know, the one you accuse of lying and being fake
But at least you don't know what is at stake
The Girl You Know who tries in every way be perfect
But even people who think they are strong fall
That Girl You Know

That Girl You Know
Or that you should, you're the one who made rumours
Did you know when you said those things
Those terrible false things that everyone believed
She was so peeved
That she relapsed, her friends and family desperate
For signs that she'll bring her walls
That Girl You Know

That Girl You Know
The one who relapsed, the one you saw collapse
The girl whom no matter how hard she tried
Couldn't die
Because her family and friends need her
Her laugh now rare
Her eyes stare
That Girl You Know

That Girl You Know
The one constantly trying to protect family and friends
Whilst wishing for her own end

The Girl You Know picking her fights
When she comes home, she cries all night
That Girl You Know
That Girl You Know
Wishes to die
To run from all her lies
The haunting ghosts of her past
Can leave her at last
That Girl You Know

That Girl You Know
Got her wish
Some might say she's selfish
Some may cry
Some may try to understand
Others would never know who she was
Some may be looking for the cause
Some might care
But I am here to say share her story if you dare
And the worst part is, if you gave her a chance
To listen and see past the 'I'm fines' and 'just tireds'
You could have saved

That Girl You Knew.

Demons

You grab me at 3pm, when I'm laughing with my friends
Or wake me up screaming at 3am from one of the nightmares
you crafted
One thought is all it takes
Before the whirlpool starts, the mistakes, the pain
The anger, the blame
Though the outside world would never know

You make me smile; you make me lie
Making me sing a chorus of 'I'm fines'
When really, I'm dying inside.
You make me restless; you make me paranoid, you
Make me overthink, you make me isolate myself
You fight me, you hit me, beat me
But no one would know because I hide it behind
Words and smiles
You obliterate my confident, self-esteem, anything that I
could
Use to fight you
You start off small with the usual
"You're useless"
You build up to crescendo when I'm too tired to fight
anymore
You hit me with the
"Why would you exist? No one will miss you, you are a
burden"

You perplex doctors and the people I know
Because you're not cold, you don't have textbook symptoms
You are an epidemic, you have killed millions, and you will

Kill millions more. Time has no limit for you, you are timeless
You are something that us mortals cannot touch.
Society hates and loves you, they hate the people who you kidnap
But love you because you are the reason they can still have authority
Over us, if the people you killed just listened to society, then they would
Have survived, the sinners that they are for getting rid of the pain, the cycle will forever continue.

You make people surrounding me think this is all for attention
You make people hate me, the quiet loner in the corner
The girl that everyone knows
I am the anomaly, how can that girl seem so normal but be in so much pain?
You made me the anomaly I am
You make me believe that I can never be loved
Because 'Who can love a girl with scars?'
You make me have bad daydreams about my deepest secrets and my deepest fears
You make me hurt myself just to forget for a second. Just for a minute.
You may hurt me, you may be killing me slowly
But no matter what, you are the one who has always been there
The one I can rely on, the one who will never leave me
The one who will never break my heart
The one who picked me up after I collapsed
The one who comforts me
Because after all, you put me through
You'll always love me
The real me
The broken me
The scarred me
The person I'll never let anyone see
Because that girl is too damaged for anyone to go near her

She'll expose herself for a few seconds, but then the walls go
back up
Because that is the way I've learned to protect myself
You are a dragon, you get angry easily, you spit fire, you
damage everything
But when you calm, like the ocean waves on a starry night,
you would protect me
From all the pain that people have caused me.

You enrage me, you make me cry, you make me feel useless
You make me hurt myself just to satisfy you
But you'll never be satisfied until I stop breathing
But I'll keep fighting you because there are thousands out
there
Battling you as I write this poem, I won't leave them, I refuse
to
I won't hurt my family or my friends
I won't spread this epidemic further; I won't give you the
power to destroy another person
You may have killed the beloved 11-year-old who was always
smiling and laughing
The 11-year-old who could talk to people without wondering
when they will leave her
My parents are still searching for that 11-year-old girl
But this 15-year-old girl will fight, she will befriend you, she
will remember what it is like
To laugh and mean it, to smile and it to be genuine, to read
and realise it isn't an escape from you, she will learn from the
pain and step out of the darkness into the light

She just needs to remember that she always has and always
will have

Demons.

Battle Scars

I went to war, I have the scars to prove it
I've counted my losses, my wounds
I watched thousands die around me
I have no army to fight you, it's me vs you
The demons will not give in, so neither will I
I am choosing life over death
I am choosing my family and friends over my demons

Blood dripping down my torso where you stabbed me in the heart
I misunderstood our conditions, you would only protect me if I agreed to
Your abuse and pain
I won't take the blame for what you've done to me
What you've made me do, people tell me that you can only trust yourself in this world
Well then, I have no one, because the biggest part of me is at war with myself
I told you that the 15-year-old would fight back for the 11-year-old that you murdered
For making me wish death when it was a miracle that I'm even alive
BAM, another lethal hit to the temple
I'm crumbling, the only thing driving me is the future
Hearing my first-born child cry
Seeing my children grow into adults
Having someone love me, the girl everyone knows, the girl with scars

SLASH, you slice my wrist where the little white marks lie
The start of this whirlpool, they are my release from the pain
you cause
I guess I never got the memo that you can't fight fire with fire
Pain with pain
That pain isn't the only feeling that is needed to make me stop
being numb
But I guess that is because you isolated me from anyone who
could help me
Seeking comfort in books, music and a corridor is all I had
against you
That was before I realised words are my shield

Seeing my little sister achieve her dreams
Seeing my brother become a doctor in genetics
Seeing my little nephew grow
Seeing my parents' love grow and grow every day
Seeing my friends less tense because I'm going to survive this
Seeing my big sister learn the trials and rewarded as a parent
Seeing my older brother fall in love, to get the job that he
wants
Seeing the relief on teachers' faces when they see me happy
again
They are my drive
And heaven help the person who goes against a girl with a
drive
Because I will live. And I will follow my dreams.

Screams fill the air; I can taste the metallic taste of blood in
my mouth
You punch me, kick me, beat me until I crumble
I can't fight anymore, I hear the feet of people, the people who
I thought left me
They defend me on the battlefield, coloured red from the
blood spilt
They pick me up, they give me a shield and sword, they fight
you. Demons.

I misunderstood, they do understand, they understand the pain, they never gave up on me
They were with me every step of the way
I was blinded by my demons
We all fight side by side, not giving up
I see my mother, my father, my brothers and sisters, I see friends and teachers alike
Fighting.
They believed in the girl that everyone knows, they supported me.
They love the girl with scars

And so can you, dear readers
I will be every step of the way, because I won't stop writing, words are my weapon
They are the source of comfort that everyone desires, they are addictive and poisonous
They can cause pain or pleasure
I will write for the people who suffer in silence
I will write for those struggling to stay afloat
I will be you sister, your friend, your confidant
I will show other boys and girls out there you can break free from the demons
You can fight them I swear
You are the anomaly that doesn't follow expectations
That is your weapon, use it, and don't stop until you are satisfied
Don't stop until you are standing strong in the sea of defeated demons

My dad tells me that I can make it, that the 11-year-old girl is still in there
He tells me to be proud of my scars, to show them to the world
Because they show that I've fought and that I made it.

He says they are my battle scars, but he is wrong

They are our battle scars.

The Day I Collapsed

I will never forget that day, four days after my birthday
But it started just a day after I turned 15
The pain, the anger, the defeat
Thursday 8th February 2018, 15:46, RE stairs
The day, the time, the place

5th February, you get to work, spreading the rumours
The lies that everyone believed
Funny how one question in biology could change everything
Of course that is not what you said
You told everyone I made our teacher change the test
Which is a lie, the one everyone believed, you told our biology table
That I slept with numerous people, another lie.
But that didn't stop you, did it?
The invisible girl in class, turned visible
You hated her for no reason.
Why, because you believed a rumour?
How low can you get, hating a person you don't know just because another girl said something?

Thursday 8th February, the big day!
I came to school, feeling anxious, scared and lonely
You waited, like a lioness stalking her prey, you told everyone on that day it was me
A girl that I talked to turned against me, she glared at me, she's angry, and I am numb.
I trusted that girl, I asked her what's wrong, she told me what I feared

I turned away from her to get my book for that lesson out of my bag, I shed a few tears
But I wiped them away.
15:30, 16 minutes to go, I'm shaky, dizzy, my demons come out to play
They see this as a golden opportunity to attack

15:40, 6 minutes, I ask to go to the toilet, the girl that I used to be friends with and the girl I used to trust followed me to the toilets, you wait for me to come out of the cubicle
The girl that I used to be friends with asked, "You here to see her?"
The girl I used to trust says "Yes"
You start your attack as soon as I step out of the toilet, telling me why I did something that didn't happen
The girl that I used to be friends with follows behind you, fuelling your anger
You tell me things I already know, I fast-walk down the F corridor trying to calm myself, fist clenched
But it's too late, I'm shaking, crying, struggling to breathe

15:46, the big moment, I get to the RE stair, I manage to climb up a couple of stairs, my legs buckle, I collapse on the stairs, I feel my heart working overtime, I feel my stomach cramp up, burning, I scream whilst I cry, the pain washes over me, my lungs can't seem to get oxygen
The demons in my head set to work to finish me off
"You are going to die, you are going to die," they chant

The girl that I used to be friends with asks if I cut myself too deep
I shake my head, unable to speak
She goes to get a teacher
The girl I used to trust, she rubs my back and tells me to try and breathe
Saying that she's such a bad person

I hated her for that, the girl who caused all this is comforting me. The irony. Making herself feel bad when I can barely breathe
"You're not!" I gasp, I comfort the girl who caused this
I couldn't tell her to let go, I scream again, this time it's my chest, the stabbing pain in my heart makes my vision go fuzzy
The girl that I used to be friends with comes back with a teacher, who asks me to try a sit-up, which is perfect, because now the girl I used to trust helps me up, the girl that I used to be friends with smiles, to the outside world it may have been reassuring but I know the difference. I know what that smile meant, this isn't over.
I later learned that my body was reacting to the fight-and-flight response, that my body was using adrenaline to get myself out of there or to fight you; of course, you know which one I chose.

I go down to the medical office, I cover for the girls, I say it's was stress for the exams
I have no idea why I did this, they should have paid for what they did, I guess I'm too nice.
The girl I used to trust stayed away for a while, but she came back and apologised. I forgave her because I am too nice.
The girl that I used to be friends with just assumed I would forgive her, that she could talk to me, that she could have my book to copy up a lesson she missed
I guessed she'd assumed I would forgive and forget.

But I won't, I will not forgive her this time, I won't forget either
I will not help her, she can work for herself for once, I'm done being little miss nice guy
I will not fight her, I dedicate this poem to her, she knows who she is, she can live with this, that she made an innocent person collapse for what?
That is all I want to know, why the rumours?
You knew that our biology teacher was never going to change the test, so what the hell did I do to you?

I've helped you with homework and classwork alike
I've never said a bad word against you until now
On the day I collapsed, I was ashamed, I felt trapped, I wasn't in control of my body and it's your fault
You people to this day still believe the rumour, but I guess that is the power of words
You made more rumours apparently when I didn't come in the next day, you said I was in the hospital getting sectioned. Another lie, I was on an art trip
You can destroy my reputation, you can hurt me, but if you go after my family, my little sister, my friends

You are going to regret that day

Like I regret the day I collapsed.

I'm Sorry

I'm Sorry for the pain I've caused, the tears you've shed over me

I'm Sorry that I make you worry, that I won't talk to you for weeks on

End, that I will ignore your texts concerned with my wellbeing

I'm Sorry that I'm not worthy of your praise, your love

I'm Sorry that I thought nobody could love me who wasn't my family

I'm Sorry that I'm failing your subject, I'm trying hard, I swear

I just wish you could understand.

I'm Sorry that I text you at 3am from a nightmare

I'm Sorry that you think that I'm useless

I'm Sorry that I allow you to keep pushing me, people think you're so nice, I guess you are

Not nice to people who are, as you called me a 'Suicidal Freak'

I'm Sorry that my life was a gift, that I was supposed to die, and now I am wasting my life

I'm Sorry that I can't forget what you did to me

I'm Sorry that I find it hard to talk to you, that I can't seem to cope in social situations

I'm Sorry that I'm not good with crowds, that I'm not the fun friend

I'm Sorry that I'm not the friend you deserve, the one that can make you laugh, the one who doesn't worry you

I'm Sorry that I can't believe anyone who can love me. I've gone through years and years of being picked on, so don't tell me anything that could possibly bring my hopes up and then crush it.

I'm Sorry that I'm not confident, that I can't walk into a room with everyone looking at me with a smile, because to the world I am invisible

I'm Sorry that I don't trust you, it's not you, I've had too many experiences of people leaving me, I just patiently wait for you to do the same

I'm Sorry that I'm not the daughter you deserve, I'm sorry I scream and shout at you, I don't mean it, I love you, Mum and Dad, just give me time

I'm Sorry that I am not the sister that you can be close with

I'm Sorry that I was hard on you, my little sister, I know you are going through a tough time, but I'll always be there for you, just hold on, I will never leave you

I'm Sorry to you, my wonderful siblings, that I shut down before you can see what's wrong

I'm Sorry that I built walls so high that the only way I can convey my feelings is through poems

I'm Sorry that I can't look you in the eye

I'm Sorry that I am not the A* student you want me to be

I'm Sorry that I listen to music, because in my eyes, music understands

I'm Sorry that I run to a corridor where I can blend in and no one will notice me.

I'm Sorry that I'm drowning, but I won't let you save me, because that means I will trust you

I'm Sorry I let you break my heart

I'm Sorry that I look back at our friendship and text you at one in the morning hoping that we can be friends again

I'm Sorry that I hurt myself, I know you are scared that I will act on my thoughts

I wish that you'd understand that I want to live but I also just want to stop existing at the same time

I'm Sorry that you don't understand me, that I won't accept your compliments, I don't know how to, my demons convinced me that I don't deserve them

I'm Sorry you think that I do this for attention, that I allowed myself to break in front of you

8th February 2018 will always be engrained into my brain, that is the day I realised what two people could do to one innocent one

I'm Sorry that I allowed you to call me disgusting things

I'm Sorry that you believed the false rumours

I'm Sorry that I will never trust you, you've lost it and you will never get it back

I'm Sorry that I will protect you, little sister, I know it must annoy you that I expect you to be as paranoid as me, to be overcautious

I'm Sorry that I can't protect you from your ears, I wish I could take you back when you were little, where we could play in the garden, where I would hug you, protect you when you were bullied, but I can't anymore, you built your walls and I've built mine

I'm Sorry I won't let you see me break down

I'm Sorry I won't let you comfort me

I broke down once and the girls who caused me to break down comforted me whilst I struggled to breathe

I won't allow myself to break down at school again

I won't allow myself to accept new people in my life

I'm Sorry that you saw me cry, that I thought you would be there for me

I'm Sorry that I showed you my scars, because that just added fuel to the fire

I'm Sorry that I allow you to talk to me, because I can't control what you will do next

I'm Sorry that my peers believed the rumours

I'm Sorry that the only person who understood my demons, who could save me from the edge, left the school

I'm Sorry that I sleep in class, I'm sorry that I struggle to sleep at night
I'm Sorry that I opened my mouth and talked
I'm Sorry that you believe in me, because ultimately it just leaves you questioning me when I fail

I'm Sorry that you think my poetry is too realistic and sensitive
It's the only way I can talk about my feelings
I'm Sorry to anyone who can relate to this poem, because it means you are going through the same pain too
I'm Sorry that I'm too nice
I'm Sorry that I allow you to walk all over me
I'm Sorry that I allow myself to do all the work and you get all the credit
I'm Sorry that you hate me for no real cause, just that I follow rules and read
I'm Sorry for saying I'm Sorry.

I'm Just Sorry.

Hush, Little Sister

Hush, Little Sister, dry your tears, the pain of today is over
I will hold you as the tears stream
I know they hurt you
Their words are like a thousand daggers in the heart
You thought it would be different here
So did I
You get bullied for something you cannot control
You get teased for not wearing makeup
Or having social media
Or the fact you don't have a boyfriend
So hush, Little Sister, I am here.

Hush, Little Sister, I know of the hate you feel towards me
The way I shut you down when you get too close
We both built our walls, our hearts like ice
Our hearts will not thaw
Our pain will not end
Some will tell us it's just life
I don't believe it's life
It is the people
They attack you with words and me with fists
So hush, Little Sister, I am here.

Hush, Little Sister, I know I scare you
I know that you hate that you can't understand
Or control my anxiety or depression
I know you wish I'd stop hurting myself
I know you wish I'd end the toxic relationships
But I accept the love I think I deserve
I know I make you cry

I know I make you scream in frustration
So hush, Little Sister, I am here.

Hush, Little Sister, put those fists down
There is no need to fight
Your eyes look for hope
You find none.
In this world of hate and war
You stand out like a beacon of hope
I know we don't open ourselves up to love
But I think you are one of the only people I truly love
So hush, Little Sister, I am here.

I remember the times we used to play with one another
When we knew no pain
No anger
The games we used to play
That once-eternal smile that shines from your face
You turn to your music, your escape from the trouble that the
world causes you
Your voice, you can hear the pain and sadness in your music
The undertones of self-doubt.
Your voice is my lullaby
It calms the worst of my storms
The worst of everything
So hush, Little Sister, I am here

My darling sister
You had gone through so much before you were even born
You went through so much pain
Through operations
Through the hospital appointments
Through seeing your older sister watch her whole world
crumble around her
Through sitting in ICU
Through the tears
Through everything you manage to be happy
You manage to laugh

To be the embodiment of hope
You are so brave
In this world of confusion, you are certain of your path
In this world of battles, you tear down your enemies with one
swoop of a sword
So hush, Little Sister, I am here

I know I can't promise you forever, because I can't keep that
promise
I know you struggle with your own mental health
I know you have pulled so many people from the edge
I know you make yourself strong even when you are weak
I know you keep your demons at bay
I admire your strength
I adore your willingness and eagerness to live
I know you lost the older sister you once adored
I know you wish I was a cooler and more stable older sister
A sister who didn't get anxious just by going outside

So hush, Little Sister, I love you
You make me want to be a better person each and every day.

Scars

They are on my wrists and thighs
They symbolise pain and destruction
They symbolise 15 years of bullying
A broken girl picked up a razor and cut
Until she bled
She remembers the satisfaction she felt
Her excuses are stupid, but you believe them

When she cries because someone touched her fresh cuts
The pain unbelievable
You tell her she deserves it
That she asked for it
Maybe she did
She thought she could trust you
That you would understand
She was wrong

Not being able to wear swimsuits
Not being able to wear short sleeves
Not telling her family
For the shame
The pain
And the fear they thought she was doing this for attention
And she was right
You don't believe in her
And it hurts

You call her a wimp for crying
That she shouldn't show her pain outwardly
She should never let anyone see her pain

So she bottles things up
She built walls
She pushed her loved ones away
Her razor was her comfort
Her pain was the only thing that didn't leave her

That girl is me
That pain is mine
You have seen me cry
And now I can't look you in the eye
I want you to understand
But you won't
You don't love me
You leave me and my scars.